Amelia Bedelia

Hops To It

Greenwillow Books, An Imprint of HarperCollins Publishers

Amelia Bedelia

Hops To It

by Herman Parish 🥚 pictures by Lynne Avril

Art was created digitally in Adobe Photoshop.
Amelia Bedelia is a registered trademark of Peppermint Partners, LLC.

Printed in the United States of America. For information address HarperCollins Children's Books, a division
of HarperCollins Publishers, 195 Broadway, New York, NY 10007.
www.harpercollinschildrens.com

Library of Congress Control Number: 2021950690
ISBN 978-0-06-296210-2 (hardback)—ISBN 978-0-06-296209-6 (paperback)

21 22 23 24 25 PC/BRR 10 9 8 7 6 5 4 3 2 1
Greenwillow Books

To Tamar Mshvildadze,
Amelia Bedelia's ambassador
to the country of Georgia—H. P.

To Sylvie, Virginia, Lois, and Herman.
We've always hopped to it!—L. A.

Amelia Bedelia

Finally

Joy

Clay

Heather

Cliff

Wade

Dawn

Skip

Angel

Penny

Candy

CONTENTS

Chapter 1: No Fool Like an April Fool 1

CHAPTER 2: "What Color Is Your
GREEN House?" 18

Chapter 3: See You Later, Incubator! 32

Chapter 4: Sit Tight or Hang Loose? 46

Chapter 5: Egg on Her Face 54

Chapter 6: Spring into Action 74

Chapter 7: An Incubator That Re-Fuses
to Die 87

Chapter 8: A Taste of Holland 94

Chapter 9: No Business Like
          Show Business . . . 111

Chapter 10: Homecoming for Harriet 123

Chapter 11: "I Don't Want to Hear
           a PEEP Out of You!" 129

Two Ways to Say It 138

Make Your Own Springtime Flowers 140

Amelia Bedelia's April Fools Sweet Sliders
and Fries 144

Amelia Bedelia Hops To It

No Fool Like an April Fool

Amelia Bedelia woke with a start and sat up in bed. Something had disturbed her, but she wasn't sure what it was. A dream? A nightmare? Sleepily, she got dressed and headed downstairs.

"Morning, cupcake," said her mother.

Amelia Bedelia smiled. "Good morning,

Mommy," she replied, rubbing her eyes. "What's for . . ." Her voice trailed off when she spotted the fried egg perched on a plate at her place at the table. The smile faded from her face.

"Breakfast is served, milady," said her father with a deep bow.

"Thank you, migentleman," said Amelia Bedelia, giving him a quick curtsy.

Amelia Bedelia sat down and gulped. How could her father forget that frying was her very least favorite way to fix an egg? Hard-boiled, soft-boiled, scrambled, poached, deviled—yes, please. She'd never ever turned down an omelet, especially if it had cheddar cheese melted in it. But fried eggs? No thank you.

She stared at the single glistening yellow yolk. *Gross.* Why were eggs like this called sunny-side up? There was nothing sunny about this egg. She began feeling a tiny bit queasy.

"Something wrong?" asked her father, sliding into his seat next to her. He was smiling and laughing, looking so pleased with himself that Amelia Bedelia did not want to complain and hurt his feelings.

"Um, no," she said. "Thanks for breakfast, Daddy." She picked up her fork, took a deep breath, and poked the yolk. To her surprise, it didn't break. She stabbed it again. Nothing. She lifted her fork, and the whole yolk came up with it.

She looked at her father. "There's something wrong with my egg," she said.

Amelia Bedelia's parents both burst out laughing. "April Fools!" said her father. "Your fried egg is actually half a canned peach on top of some vanilla yogurt!"

"Really?" said Amelia Bedelia. She took a bite. Then another. It was delicious.

Her mother shook her head. "Didn't you hear me shriek this morning when I took my first sip of coffee?" she asked.

"Oh! *That's* what woke me up!" said Amelia Bedelia.

Her father looked embarrassed. "I put salt in the sugar bowl," he confessed. "An April Fools' Day classic. Sorry. I couldn't resist."

Amelia Bedelia shook her head. "Oh, Daddy," she said.

April Fools' Day was Amelia Bedelia's father's favorite holiday. He was always coming up with new tricks to play on his family. Last year he'd filled a bowl halfway with milk, stuck a spoon in it, and put it in the freezer overnight. The next morning, he poured some cereal and milk on top and served it to Amelia Bedelia. She was so confused when she couldn't budge the spoon, no matter how hard she tried.

Amelia Bedelia's father stood up and kissed the top of her head. "You really were going to take a bite of your least-favorite breakfast just for me, weren't you?"

Amelia Bedelia nodded.

"Your heart is always in the right place, honey bun," said her mother.

Amelia Bedelia placed her hand on her chest. "I hope so," she replied.

Spring was in the air as Amelia Bedelia walked to school that morning. The sun was shining, birds were singing, trees were budding, flowers were blooming, and bees were buzzing.

Amelia Bedelia skipped for the entire last block. She bounced past Oak Tree Elementary's custodian, Mr. Jack, who was trimming the bushes in front of the building. "The hedges are getting their first haircut of the year," said Amelia Bedelia.

Mr. Jack smiled. "Don't you have a

spring in your step this morning!" he said.

"No springs," said Amelia Bedelia. "Just new sneakers!"

Amelia Bedelia walked down the hall to her classroom, because skipping was not allowed inside. Her teacher, Mrs. Shauk, was super strict about rules. Students called her the Hawk because she never missed anything. Kids swore she had eyes in the back of her head. Amelia Bedelia was pretty sure that wasn't true, even though she herself had been caught by Mrs. Shauk when her back was turned.

Once everyone had settled into their seats, Mrs. Shauk said, "I hope that you all remembered to bring in your permission slips for the field trip to Seven Gables Farm tomorrow."

After she collected and counted them all, she smiled.

So far, so good, thought Amelia Bedelia.

"Thank you," said Mrs. Shauk. "Okay, now we are going to start our day with a little pop quiz."

Amelia Bedelia changed her mind. *So far, so bad.*

The class groaned. Amelia Bedelia began to list different flavors of soda in her head so that she'd be ready for the quiz about pop. *Orange, grape, cherry* . . .

"Take out your pencils, please," said Mrs. Shauk. She began walking up and down the aisles, placing a sheet of paper facedown on each student's desk. "This is a timed test," she informed them. "The student who finishes first *correctly* will win a prize."

Root beer, lemon-lime, ginger ale . . . Amelia Bedelia's thoughts were interrupted by Mrs. Shauk's next words. "Okay, you may turn your papers over now."

The room was silent as everyone flipped over their quizzes. Amelia Bedelia's friends got right to work. She could hear their pencils scratching out answers.

Amelia Bedelia stared down at her quiz. It was a single sheet of paper with instructions at the top and a numbered list. Though her impulse was to get started immediately like everyone else, she forced herself to slow down. *Take your time, Amelia Bedelia,* she told herself. She began to read the test and quickly discovered that Mrs. Shauk had been fooling them. This wasn't a pop quiz at all. There wasn't a single question about soda.

This is a test to see how well you follow directions. A prize will be given to the student who completes it both quickly and accurately. But please don't rush! Take your time and be thorough.

Read every question on this page before you begin.

1. Write your name on the top left-hand corner of the page.

2. Turn the paper over and write your birth date.

3. What is 5 times 42? Write your answer here _____

4. Stand up and say, "My name is _____ and I am the best at following directions."

5. On the bottom right-hand corner of the page, write your name backward.

6. Draw twelve circles on the back of this paper.

7. Now draw a smiley face in each circle.

8. Add 465 and 123. Write your answer here _____

9. Draw a line through each smiley face on the back of this page.

10. Stand up, touch your toes, and sit back down.

11. Sing the happy birthday song as fast as you can.

12. Underline the word "the" every time it appears in this quiz.

13. Clap your hands three times.

14. Answer question ~~~~~~~~~~~~~~~~~~~~~~~~~~~~~~ you are done.

While Amelia Bedelia was tempted to ignore the sentence at the top and start writing her answers immediately (especially when it was clear that Cliff was already at number five when he jumped up and shouted, "My name is Cliff, and I am the best at following directions!"), she was glad she had followed the directions when she finally got to number fourteen:

14. Answer question one and turn your paper over. You are done.

Amelia Bedelia gasped. Mrs. Shauk was playing an April Fools' trick on them! Trying not to laugh, she wrote her name in the top left-hand corner of the paper, turned it over, and folded her hands on her desk. Mrs. Shauk smiled and winked at her.

All around the room, her classmates continued to work on the quiz. They were drawing circles, adding and multiplying numbers, standing up and shouting, and singing really fast.

"Class," Mrs. Shauk finally said. "I need to interrupt you for a moment. Amelia Bedelia, will you please show everyone your paper?"

Amelia Bedelia held it up.

"You are the winner!" Mrs. Shauk proclaimed.

"Impossible!" said Clay, squinting at Amelia Bedelia's quiz. "She didn't even get to the smiley faces!"

"And she didn't sing Happy Birthday really fast yet!" added Holly.

"You were in such a rush to win, you forgot the most important part of any assignment—to follow ALL the directions," said Mrs. Shauk. "You were supposed to read the entire page before you started. Look at number fourteen."

After a moment, Amelia Bedelia's friends all said, "Ohhhhhhhhhh . . ." Many of them looked embarrassed.

"And it's too bad," said Mrs. Shauk. "Because this quiz will be fifty percent of your grade this term and—"

Holly's hand shot up. "What?" she said. "Fifty percent?"

"All because you forgot to follow directions," Mrs. Shauk continued. "And here's something else most of you forgot." She paused. "Today is April Fools' Day!"

There was a moment of silence, and then everyone burst out laughing.

"You got us good, Mrs. Shauk!" said Teddy.

"I certainly did," said Mrs. Shauk, looking quite pleased.

"What Color Is Your *GREEN* House?"

"Good morning, all! Welcome to Seven Gables Farm. It's so nice of you to *turnip*! We are the Hawthornes. This farm has been in our family for five generations, which is a really big *dill*!" It was a warm spring morning, and Mrs. Hawthorne shaded her eyes from the sun as she spoke to Amelia Bedelia and her friends. "We're a tiny organic farm, and we love to provide the community with fresh fruits, vegetables, eggs, baked goods, and flowers. We wake up at the *quack* of dawn to take care of our plants and animals. But we've set aside some *thyme* for you today, so *lettuce* show you around!"

Mr. Hawthorne nodded. "Welcome, and please follow me," he said.

As Amelia Bedelia and her classmates followed Mr. Hawthorne down a dirt path, Mrs. Shauk chuckled and turned to Ms. Garcia with a smile. "I adore Mrs. Hawthorne's silly puns!" she said.

"They're beyond *corny*, all right,"

replied Ms. Garcia. "But they still make me laugh!"

Amelia Bedelia and her friends had visited Seven Gables Farm before, tagging along with their parents on weekends to buy fresh produce and flowers from the farm stand, picking peaches in summer and apples in the fall, and enjoying cider doughnuts year-round. And, of course, going on the farm's famous haunted hayride on Halloween! But today was different. They were getting a behind-the-scenes look at how a small family farm worked.

"Do you think we'll see any baby animals today?" Amelia Bedelia asked Daisy.

Daisy shrugged. "Search me," she said.

"Why, do you have a baby bunny in your pocket?" Amelia Bedelia asked.

Daisy shook her head. "Nope," she said. "But I wish I did!"

Mr. Hawthorne came to a stop in front of a glass building. "Spring is the busiest time of year for farmers," he said. "To have a successful growing season, you need to have all of your ducks in a row."

"That must be really hard," Amelia Bedelia whispered to Daisy. "Everyone knows ducks don't like to stand still for very long."

"You see this greenhouse?" continued Mr. Hawthorne. "It's where we—"

Amelia Bedelia raised her hand. "No,

I don't see it," she said, shaking her head.

"It's right behind me," said Mr. Hawthorne. He stuck out his thumb and motioned over his shoulder like a hitchhiker.

Amelia Bedelia kept looking around. "Where?" she asked.

Mr. Hawthorne turned and pointed at the glass building behind him. "Right there," he said.

"Oh, in that case, you should definitely call it something else," said Amelia Bedelia. "Because it isn't green. It's made of shiny aluminum and glass. I can see right through it."

Mr. Hawthorne laughed. "Ah, Amelia Bedelia, you're always such a kidder, just like

I mean that literally!" She gave shovels to some of the students and showed them how to loosen the soil, breaking up clumps of earth and pulling out weeds. There weren't enough shovels to go around, so Amelia Bedelia and her friends took turns.

"I hope you are all able to pull your weight!" said Mr. Hawthorne with a smile.

Amelia Bedelia couldn't remember how much she weighed. She looked around for some rope, but all she saw were shovels.

"Your turn," said Pat, handing Amelia Bedelia his shovel. She began hacking away at the ground until *CLANG*! She hit something so hard it made her arms tingle.

"Amelia Bedelia, you struck pay dirt!" said Mrs. Hawthorne with a laugh.

Pay dirt? Amelia Bedelia smiled. Had she discovered buried treasure like she had at the shore? She kept digging. Unfortunately, her treasure turned out to be just a big rock. She was disappointed, but not for long. Once they had planted all the corn seeds, Mrs. Hawthorne had a reward for them. "You have all proven yourselves to be outstanding in your field," she said. "So how about some ice-cold lemonade?"

"Yes, please!" said Amelia Bedelia. She was so thirsty she drank two cups.

"Amelia Bedelia, you must have a hollow leg!" said Mr. Hawthorne, filling her cup again.

"Oh, I don't think so," said Amelia Bedelia. "I'm just really thirsty."

"Now *romaine* calm," said Mrs. Hawthorne when everyone had drunk their fill. "We're going to end our farm tour with a visit to the barn to see the baby animals."

There were fluffy bunnies to feed dandelion leaves to, and sweet yellow chicks to admire. The ducklings made little quacking sounds, and the baby goats all crowded around Amelia Bedelia and her friends, eager to be petted. And everyone loved the two baby donkeys with their

big brown eyes and long eyelashes! They were so new they didn't even have names yet.

"Class, it is time for us to return to school," Mrs. Shauk finally announced. "Let's give a round of applause to Mr. and Mrs. Hawthorne. They really bent over backward for us today."

Amelia Bedelia looked at Holly. "Did you see them do that?" she asked. She had had no idea that the Hawthornes were gymnasts as well as farmers! Maybe that was what Mr. Hawthorne had meant when he said that a farmer had to be flexible.

As the class began to line up to get back on the bus, Mrs. Hawthorne posed a question. "Ms. Garcia, have you ever thought about hatching eggs in your science class?" she asked. "I could provide you with the eggs, and when the chicks get too big for you, we would take them back. That way they'd have a good home, and your students could visit them whenever they wanted to."

"Oh, what a great idea!" said Ms. Garcia. "And I just saw an incubator in the storage room at school." She turned to Amelia Bedelia and her friends. "Class, a show of hands, please. Who would like to hatch baby chicks in science class?"

Every hand shot up. Amelia Bedelia wasn't taking any chances, so she showed Ms. Garcia both of hers.

"Wonderful!" said Mrs. Hawthorne. "This is going to be your best school project yet. No *yolking* around!"

See You Later, Incubator!

The next morning, Amelia Bedelia bounded down the stairs, raced into the kitchen, and plopped down at the table, a big smile on her face.

Amelia Bedelia's father looked up from his newspaper. "Good morning, sunshine," he said. "You look as happy as a clam."

Amelia Bedelia shook her head. "Oh, Daddy. How can you tell if a clam is happy or not?" she asked.

Her father thought for a moment. "Good point. There's no way to tell. Especially if it clams up. So what's going on? Why are you so happy?"

"We start our chick-hatching unit in science today. We'll learn how to take care of the eggs when they're delivered tomorrow!" Amelia Bedelia announced.

"How exciting!" said her mother.

"Well, you know what they say . . . don't count your chickens before they're hatched," her father joked, turning to the sports page.

Amelia Bedelia grabbed a piece of

buttered toast. "There won't be any chickens to count, Daddy. Just eggs!"

When Amelia Bedelia arrived at school, her friends were as excited as she was. She hung her jacket in the closet and walked to her desk.

"I can't believe this is happening," squealed Rose, bouncing in her chair. "I'm on pins and needles!"

Amelia Bedelia grabbed Rose's arm. "Quick! Stand up!"

Rose hopped to her feet and spun in a circle. "I'm so excited!" she said.

"Me too!" said Penny.

"Me three!" said Amelia Bedelia.

"Okay, everyone!" said Mrs. Shauk,

walking to the front of the room. "I know you are all excited about the chicks, but it's time to sit down and begin our day. Please take out your math notebooks. Let's start with some word problems."

Once everyone had their pencils out and notebooks opened, Mrs. Shauk said, "Bob owns the Big Dipper Ice Cream Shop. One day he sold one hundred and three scoops of chocolate chip, fifty-five scoops of fudge ripple, and seventy-three scoops of pink bubblegum. How many scoops of ice cream did he sell in all?"

The class stared back at her.

"Anyone?" Mrs. Shauk asked.

Skip looked down at his notebook. "Um, a lot?" he said.

Mrs. Shauk sighed and walked to the whiteboard. She uncapped her pen and was about to start writing when she turned back around to the class with a smile. "Let's try a different approach," she said. "Bob owns the Happy Acres Chicken Farm. He has one hundred and three hens, fifty-five roosters, and seventy-three chicks. How many chickens does he have in all?"

After a moment, almost everyone's hand shot up.

"Yes, Heather?" said Mrs. Shauk.

"Two hundred and thirty-one!" Heather said.

"Excellent!" said Mrs. Shauk.

The rest of the word problems that morning featured Bob and his chickens. Amelia Bedelia and her friends got them all right, and in record time too.

"Nicely done, class," said Mrs. Shauk. She looked very pleased.

Clay raised his hand.

"Yes, Clay?" said Mrs. Shauk.

"Why do chickens lay eggs?" he asked.

Mrs. Shauk nodded. "That's a good question," she said. "There are two reasons. One, to hatch baby chicks. And two, for people to eat." She smiled.

As long as they're not fried, thought Amelia Bedelia.

Clay grinned. "Actually," he said,

"chickens lay eggs because if they dropped them, they'd break!"

Mrs. Shauk looked stern for a moment. Then she laughed. "I can't argue with you there, Clay," she said.

After math class was over, Amelia Bedelia and her friends trooped into Ms. Garcia's classroom. The incubator, a large plastic oval with a see-through top, sat on a table at the front of the room. It reminded Amelia Bedelia of a small flying saucer, like in those old black-and-white movies about alien invaders that her father liked to watch.

Everyone gathered around the incubator excitedly. Soon it would be filled with eggs, which would soon be filled with growing chicks, pecking their way out of their shells to become living, breathing chickens. Sure, they had Hermione the corn snake and Harriet the hamster in their science classroom, but this was different.

"I've never seen you so eager for science class!" said Ms. Garcia. "I have to admit, I'm pretty excited too."

"But are you *eggcited*?" asked Clay.

Ms. Garcia laughed. "I am!"

Once everyone was settled, Ms. Garcia said, "As you all know, we are about to start a new unit where we will be incubating and hatching baby chicks in our classroom. This is a very important job. We need to keep the eggs moist and warm, so we'll have to monitor the temperature and the humidity of the incubator. Plus, the developing chicks need to be positioned correctly inside their shells, so we'll be rotating the eggs three times a day. And we'll be keeping track of everything we do and recording our observations in these egg hatching journals." She held up a stack of journals, each with a fuzzy chick on the cover, and began handing them out to the class. Amelia Bedelia took out her favorite pen and wrote her name very carefully and neatly on the front of hers.

"So, what can you tell me about chickens?" Ms. Garcia asked.

"They have beaks and floppy red

thingamabobs on their heads," said Penny.

"Combs," said Ms. Garcia.

"Chickens don't need combs," said Amelia Bedelia. "They don't have hair."

"That's right," said Wade. "They have feathers. But they can't really fly very far."

"Anything else?" said Mrs. Garcia.

"They are called fowl," said Joy.

"Foul?" Amelia Bedelia asked. That couldn't be right. Chickens were so friendly, nice, and sweet, plus they didn't play sports!

Ms. Garcia nodded. "Yes, fowl," she said. "They are in the same scientific order as turkeys and pheasants."

"Well, I'd rather call them chickens," said Amelia Bedelia.

"Chickens are smart and have excellent memories," said Ms. Garcia. "And believe it or not, they are descended from dinosaurs!"

"No way!" said Chip.

Ms. Garcia nodded. "Chickens are the closest living relative we have to the *T. rex*." She paused. "Anything else you can tell me about them?" She turned to look at the incubator. "We left out a pretty important fact."

"Oh," said Amelia Bedelia. "They lay eggs!"

"That's right," said Ms. Garcia. "After we set up the incubator, I'm going to pick up the eggs from Mrs. Hawthorne. Then we will label them and place them inside very carefully. We'll have to keep track

and make sure to rotate them three times a day. Can anyone guess how long it will take for the chicks to hatch?" she asked.

"Um, nine months?" Teddy guessed.

"Chicks grow much faster than human babies," Ms. Garcia said. "It will take only twenty-one days for them to hatch from the time they start incubating. So, is everyone ready?"

Amelia Bedelia and her friends cheered. Ms. Garcia smiled and picked up the incubator's cord. Cliff began a shortened countdown that added to the suspense. "Five, four, three . . ." Ms. Garcia carefully inserted the prongs of the plug into the outlet on the wall. "Two, one . . . BLASTOFF!" The incubator lit up and glowed, humming with a static buzz that grew louder and louder. The students cheered again. Suddenly there was a flash of light and a loud *POP*!

"Uh-oh," said Ms. Garcia. "We do not have liftoff!"

Sit Tight or Hang Loose?

few seconds later, Mr. Jack was on
the scene. "Everybody okay?" he asked.
"Anybody hurt?" After making sure that
everyone was fine and it was safe, he
carefully unplugged the incubator.

Ms. Garcia sighed. "Well, that was a
disappointment," she said.

"The school bought this incubator right after I started working here," said Mr. Jack. "I put it together. We go back a long way."

"Oh, so it was ancient," said Ms. Garcia. "And on its last legs."

"Well, I don't know about that," said Mr. Jack, picking up the incubator and tucking it under his arm. "I think we've both got some life left in us."

Amelia Bedelia looked around the classroom. She wondered if she was the only one paying attention to this odd conversation.

Ms. Chase, the gym teacher, stuck her head in the doorway. "Is everything okay?" she asked. "What was that noise?"

"Our incubator gave up the ghost," said Ms. Garcia. "Dead as a doornail."

Amelia Bedelia's eyes widened. She looked at her friends. Was the incubator haunted? Could they get new legs for it?

Ms. Garcia thought for a moment. "Would you mind keeping an eye on the class?" she asked Ms. Chase.

That sounded pretty uncomfortable to Amelia Bedelia, but to her surprise, Ms. Chase agreed.

Ms. Garcia turned to the students. "Can you all sit tight while I'm gone?"

They nodded. Amelia Bedelia shifted in her seat. How did you sit tight? And how was it different from the way she usually sat? She looked around at her friends.

Everyone looked exactly the same, only more worried. The classroom was quiet.

"I'll be back in a few minutes," said Ms. Garcia. "Hang loose till then."

Amelia Bedelia was confused. Should she sit tight or hang loose? What was the difference?

"So . . . um . . . how do chickens stay in shape?" Clay asked.

"I don't know, Clay," Ms. Chase finally said. "How *do* chickens stay in shape?"

"They *egg*cercise," answered Clay.

"Well, I should have known that one," said the gym teacher.

A few kids laughed half-heartedly.

"Why did the chicken cross the playground?" Clay asked. "To get to the

other slide! What do you call a chicken that goes on safari? An eggsplorer!"

Even though Amelia Bedelia thought Clay's jokes were pretty good, she was too worried to even smile.

"What did the egg say to the clown?" Clay continued.

"You crack me up," came the answer from the doorway. Ms. Garcia had returned. She thanked Ms. Chase and then sat down at her desk.

"I just went to Principal Hotchkiss's office and told her what happened," she explained. "I asked her if there was any money in the budget to purchase a new incubator."

"And what did she say?" asked Teddy.

Ms. Garcia shook her head. "It seems the school is strapped for cash."

"Is that good or bad?" asked Amelia Bedelia.

Candy turned around in her seat. "They're out of dough," she said.

"So, no more Pizza Fridays?" said Amelia Bedelia. "What does that have to do with the baby chicks?"

"It means that there's simply no extra money for a new incubator," Ms. Garcia explained. She shook her head sadly. "It looks like we're not going to be able to hatch chicks after all."

"*Awwwwww,*" the class groaned.

"I'm sorry," said Ms. Garcia. "I know how disappointing this is."

Amelia Bedelia and her friends sat in stunned silence.

Until, all of a sudden, Amelia Bedelia started to laugh.

"What's so funny?" asked Ms. Garcia.

"You fooled us, Ms. Garcia," Amelia Bedelia said.

"Did I?" asked Ms. Garcia.

"It's a late April Fools' joke, right?" said Amelia Bedelia.

Ms. Garcia sighed. "I really wish I was joking," she said.

"Me too," said Amelia Bedelia, her eyes wide.

Not even Clay had anything funny to say after that.

Egg on Her Face

"I'm sorry for the disappointment about the chicks," Ms. Garcia said the next day. "But as we all know, the show must go on."

That perked Amelia Bedelia up. A show would be a terrific way to cheer up the class! Everyone was still so sad about not hatching eggs in science.

"We're going to make rubber eggs!" Ms. Garcia continued. "It's a great way to learn about the parts of an egg. And it's super fun too." She pointed to the whiteboard, where she had drawn a cross section of an egg.

It wasn't really a show, but it sounded interesting to Amelia Bedelia just the same. Plus, the project would take several days. First Ms. Garcia gave everyone an empty jar and a brown egg. They carefully placed their eggs inside their jars, then poured in enough white vinegar to cover the egg. Then they added one drop of food coloring and gently mixed it.

"Do your eggs look any different?" Ms. Garcia asked, a day later.

Amelia Bedelia had chosen to add a drop of red food coloring to her vinegar the day before. Now there was a layer of foam on the surface of the vinegar, and some larger, darker thin pieces floating in the jar. She carefully lifted the egg out of the jar with a spoon. Her egg was a pretty shade of pink, and the surface was speckled. She gently poked it.

"My egg is starting to get soft!" she cried.

Ms. Garcia nodded. "The shell is dissolving. It is made of calcium carbonate," she explained. "And vinegar is a weak acid. When the calcium carbonate and the vinegar combine, it causes a chemical reaction. The calcium dissolves and floats off the egg. You can see the bigger pieces floating in the jar. And the carbonate creates carbon dioxide. That's the foamy bubbles that you see."

On Monday, the eggs were ready.

"Now carefully remove your eggs from the vinegar," said Ms. Garcia. "We're going to take turns gently rinsing the eggs to make sure all the shell is gone."

Amelia Bedelia held the egg in her hand. It felt slimy and squishy, but solid.

"But how come there's no shell but it's still shaped like an egg?" asked Skip.

"Great question, Skip," said Ms. Garcia.

"There are two membranes inside the shell—the inner and outer membranes. They hold the contents of the egg in place. The membranes protect the egg from bacteria and keep the moisture levels balanced inside. They are mainly made of protein. That's why they did not dissolve in the vinegar."

Amelia Bedelia raised her hand. "Is it my imagination, or did my egg get bigger?"

"Good observation," said Ms. Garcia. "The eggs did get bigger. The water in the vinegar passed through the membranes to equalize the concentration of water on the inside and the outside of the egg. This process is called osmosis."

"I can see inside my egg!" Wade said.

"That's right," said Ms. Garcia. "Without the shell, the egg is now translucent. Let's take a closer look at what's inside."

Everyone held up their eggs to the light.

"The round part in the middle is the yolk, which provides food for the growing chick. The yolk is surrounded by the egg white, also called albumen, which is what the chick grows in. It provides protein and water. Now in some of your eggs, you may be able to see cords on either side of the yolk. They are called the chalazae, and they hold the yolk in place in the center of the shell, so it is protected."

"The *what*-lazy?" asked Amelia Bedelia.

"The kah-LAY-zee," said Ms. Garcia slowly.

"Very cool," said Dawn.

"And now we have rubber eggs!" said Ms. Garcia. She bounced her egg gently on her desk. "Don't squeeze it too hard, though."

"Even cooler!" Dawn whispered.

Amelia Bedelia carefully bounced her pink egg on her desk. It really did bounce! She gently squeezed it, enjoying its rubbery smoothness.

"Hey, Amelia Bedelia!" said Cliff. "Look inside my egg!" He held it up close to her face so she could take a look.

"Be careful, Cliff," warned Ms. Garcia.

"These eggs are very delica—"

SPLOOSH! The egg broke open in Cliff's hand. Amelia Bedelia was splashed with a face full of egg goo.

"*EWWWW! Gross!*" Amelia Bedelia shuddered.

"I'm really, really sorry, Amelia Bedelia," said Cliff. "You're not the only one with egg on your face! I was sure it wouldn't break, and look what happened."

"Are you sure? I don't see any egg on your face," said Amelia Bedelia.

"You can both wash up at the sink," said Ms. Garcia. "But before you do, I just wanted to point out to everyone that the white part of the egg has been dyed by the food coloring, but the yolk is still its normal color, because it has another special membrane around it."

Amelia Bedelia headed to the sink in the back of the room. She wet some paper towels and began to scrub. It took a while to get the egg off her face and out of her hair.

When she was done, Ms. Garcia called. "Amelia Bedelia, I forgot to freshen Hermione's and Harriet's water this morning. Would you mind taking care of that?"

"Yes," said Amelia Bedelia. "Um, I mean no, I wouldn't mind." She lifted the top of Hermione's cage. The pretty orange-and-red-patterned snake picked up her head and flicked her tongue at Amelia Bedelia. Amelia Bedelia flicked hers right back. She rinsed Hermione's bowl, filled it with fresh water, and placed it back in the cage.

But when Amelia Bedelia reached for the door to Harriet's cage, it opened way too easily. She realized it wasn't fastened properly—not only that, she didn't see Harriet. "Harriet, where are you?" she called softly. But Harriet wasn't on her hamster wheel or in her little house. Was she hiding in the corner of the cage? Amelia Bedelia gently poked at the pile of hay and shavings, hoping to find the hamster.

"Ms. Garcia!" she cried.

Ms. Garcia rushed to the back of the room. "What's wrong?' she asked.

"It's Harriet!" Amelia Bedelia said. "She's gone!"

Amelia Bedelia and her friends stood quietly around the tree-stump table. At recess, they usually scattered, heading for the swings, the foursquare court, the jungle gym, a game of soccer. But today no one seemed to be in the mood.

"Poor Ms. Garcia," said Dawn. "First the incubator breaks, and now this."

Amelia Bedelia sighed. They had spent the rest of science class carefully moving books off shelves, searching every desk, closet, and cupboard. But there was no sign of Harriet anywhere.

"Ms. Garcia didn't seem too upset," said Daisy. "She said that Harriet probably had spring fever."

"Oh no," said Amelia Bedelia. "Even worse! Harriet is missing *and* sick!"

"I think she'll be okay," said Angel. "Ms. Garcia is going to leave food on the classroom floor tonight, and she said that Harriet will probably be back in the morning."

"Well, let's all keep our fingers crossed that she comes home soon," said Dawn, "and that we somehow get a new incubator. Then everything will be back to normal."

"But Mrs. Hotchkiss said there isn't any money," Daisy reminded everyone.

Pat jumped on top of the tree stump and raised his fist in the air. "We can't take this lying down!" he said. "It is our right as students of Oak Tree Elementary to hatch baby chicks in our classroom!"

"Pat," said Amelia Bedelia, laughing. "You're not lying down, you're standing up!"

Penny nodded. "He is standing up for what's right," she said. "We were so excited to hatch chicks. It isn't fair."

"Maybe we could all chip in for a new incubator?" suggested Skip. He reached into his pocket and pulled out a penny, two nickels, and an unwrapped piece of gum. It was fuzzy with lint.

Chip shook his head. "That's not going to cut it," he said.

"And it's definitely not enough either," added Amelia Bedelia. "Incubators must be expensive."

"Should we ask our parents for the money?" asked Wade.

"I don't know," said Angel softly. "Wouldn't it be great if we could raise the money ourselves? Ms. Garcia would be so proud of us."

"My big sister is in the marching band. Last year they wanted to go to a competition in another state," Joy said. "So they had a fundraiser."

"That's a great idea! We could do that," said Cliff.

"But like what, exactly?" asked Teddy.

"Like a bake sale or a road race or something," said Holly. "My sister's debate team did a danceathon. They got pledges from people and danced all night and made all the money they needed."

"That's way too much dancing," said Teddy. "How about we sell tickets to something. I know—we could put on a play! Then the whole town could come."

Penny shook her head. "It would be fun, but I don't think we have enough time," she said. "We need the incubator soon!"

Amelia Bedelia thought about the broken incubator. That made her think of baby chicks, which made her think about bunnies, which led to egg hunts.

"That's it!" said Amelia Bedelia. "Let's have a spring fair right here at school. And invite the whole town. We could sell tickets and there could be an egg hunt and a parade where everyone wears funny hats!"

"And a bake sale!" said Angel.

Naturally, Candy suggested something that involved candy. "I'll get a huge jar and fill it with jelly beans, and people can buy chances to guess how many are inside. Whoever guesses closest wins the whole thing," she said.

"We could have fun games," said Skip. "Like an egg-and-spoon race or a ring toss."

"Or an egg toss!" said Angel. "You back up one step with every toss until the egg breaks as someone tries to catch it."

"And how about an obstacle course? We could call it the Bunny Hop," said Cliff.

"Kids could wear fluffy ears and tails and have to hop the whole way," said Clay.

Amelia Bedelia jumped up. "What great ideas!" she said. "I know, let's have a petting zoo with baby animals. Maybe Mrs. Hawthorne would help us. I bet Mr. Jack will help too."

Joy whipped out a notebook and started taking notes. When she was done, everyone had an assignment.

Cliff and Clay: Obstacle Course
Heather and Holly: Bake Sale
Dawn and Rose: Egg Hunt
Amelia Bedelia: Petting Zoo and Talk to Mr. Jack
Angel: Posters
Candy: Candy for Egg Hunt and Jelly Bean Count
Penny, Daisy, Wade, Skip, and Pat: Carnival Games
Chip and Teddy: Funny Hat Parade

"That just leaves me," Joy said. She sighed. "I guess I'll get the ball rolling by getting permission from Mrs. Hotchkiss."

"Do not bring a ball," said Amelia Bedelia. "Mrs. Hotchkiss doesn't allow them in the hallways."

"Oh, I won't," Joy said. "I don't want to get off on the wrong foot with her."

Amelia Bedelia looked down at Joy's feet. "I can't tell the difference between the right one and the wrong one," she said. "But I really like your sneakers!"

Spring into Action

Approval was granted. A date was chosen. Angel designed a great poster, which Mrs. Roman made into stacks of copies. Things were falling into place. Harriet the hamster, was still missing, but Ms. Garcia was hopeful. She put out food before she left the science room each

Egg Hunt!

Come One! Come All!

Bunny Hop Obstacle Course

to the

OAK TREE ELEMENTARY

Spring Fair

Egg-StraVagaNZa

Bake Sale

This Saturday

Carnival Games

12:00-3:00PM

Petting Zoo

Fun for all ages!!!

Funny Hat Parade

$5 Admission

night, and every morning it was gone. So they all knew that Harriet was nearby. "She's on a little vacation," Ms. Garcia told the class. "She'll be back when she's ready."

After school, Amelia Bedelia and her friends headed into town to put up posters and round up donations. Clay and Cliff were going to Petal Pushers Gardening Store to see if they could get some props for the obstacle course. Dawn and Rose were headed to I'm Crafty to see if they had any plastic eggs to donate for the egg hunt. Candy was off to Toot Sweet Confections hoping to get donated candy to fill the eggs. Cliff, Clay, Chip, and Teddy hit up the Mask-querade Costume Shop for extra bunny ears, cotton tails, and unusual hats. Heather and Holly asked Pete of Pete's Diner if he'd like to donate some baked goods.

Amelia Bedelia had left a message for Mrs. Hawthorne, asking about baby animals for the petting zoo. Now she was waiting to hear back.

As Amelia Bedelia stapled a poster to the big bulletin board outside the supermarket, she heard someone say, "A spring fair? How enchanting!"

Amelia Bedelia turned around. "Hi, Mrs. Larkin!" she said. Amelia Bedelia and her friends had once helped save Mrs. Larkin's cat, Cinnamon.

"I'll be there!" said Mrs. Larkin.

"Thanks!" said Amelia Bedelia. Just then she remembered Mrs. Larkin's delicious pumpkin pies. "Would you like to contribute goodies for our bake sale?" she said brightly.

"I'd be pleased as punch," said Mrs. Larkin. "I'll bake cupcakes!"

"Oh, thank you," said Amelia Bedelia. "I'll put you down for punch and cupcakes."

Mrs. Larkin looked slightly confused as she wheeled her cart into the store.

Amelia Bedelia waved, then headed off to put up more posters on lampposts, electrical poles, and other likely places—the library, Perfect Pizza Parlor, Last

Licks Ice Cream Shoppe, and Paw Palace pet store.

When she passed the animal shelter a couple of blocks away, Amelia Bedelia decided to go in to hang a poster and say hello to Dr. Wiggins. Dr. Wiggins was a retired veterinarian who ran the shelter and had helped Amelia Bedelia adopt her dog, Finally.

The shelter was the noisiest place in town. When Amelia Bedelia pushed open the door, it was even louder than usual.

Arf! Arf! Arf! Ruff! Ruff! Aroooooooooo!

"Hello, Ms. Crabtree," she said to the receptionist.

Ms. Crabtree did not look up.

"Um, hello!" Amelia Bedelia said, louder this time.

Ms. Crabtree jumped. "Oh, Amelia Bedelia!" she said. "Sorry, it's so noisy in here! I think I'm going to lose my marbles."

"Don't worry," replied Amelia Bedelia. "You can get more at the toy store."

Arf! Arf! Ruff! Arooooooooooo! Arf! Arf!

Amelia Bedelia held up a poster, then pointed to the bulletin board. Ms. Crabtree gave her a thumbs-up.

When the poster was in place, Amelia Bedelia asked, "Is Dr. Wiggins here?"

Just then, Dr. Wiggins came out holding a wriggly black-and-white puppy. The barking began again.

Arf! Arf! Arf! Ruff! Arooooooooooo!

Dr. Wiggins handed the puppy to Ms. Crabtree. She gestured to the door, and she and Amelia Bedelia headed outside.

"It's nice to see you, Amelia Bedelia," Dr. Wiggins said. "Sorry about the noise. We have twice as many puppies as usual. We're swamped!"

"Maybe you should call a plumber!" said Amelia Bedelia.

"I did call for extra volunteers," said Dr. Wiggins.

"You are so devoted to your puppies," said Amelia Bedelia.

Dr. Wiggins laughed. "Dedication is my middle name."

"It is?" asked Amelia Bedelia.

Dr. Wiggins sighed. "I'm worried about finding homes for all these puppies. Can you spread the word?"

"I'm not sure how to do that," said Amelia Bedelia. "But I can let everyone know."

"Great," said Dr. Wiggins. "What do you have there?"

Amelia Bedelia handed her a flyer for the spring fair.

"What a wonderful idea," said Dr. Wiggins. "I wish I could help, but I'm just too busy. I will stop by, though."

After she said goodbye to Dr. Wiggins, Amelia Bedelia met her friends in front of the library. The afternoon was a success. The posters were all up. They had bunny ears, cotton tails, funny hats, eggs to fill, and candy to fill them with. Pete was going to donate doughnuts and lemonade. Mrs. Larkin was bringing cupcakes and punch.

"This is so *egg*citing!" said Clay.

"I *egg*spect that Ms. Garcia will be beside herself when she finds out," said Cliff.

"That's impossible," said Amelia Bedelia. "But she'll be really happy!"

When Amelia Bedelia got home, the telephone was ringing. She took off her backpack and set it on the floor.

"Oh, good, you're home," said her mother, handing her the phone. "It's Mrs. Hawthorne."

"Hello, Amelia Bedelia," said Mrs. Hawthorne. "It was *udderly* great to hear your voice on my answering machine!"

"Thanks for calling back, Mrs. Hawthorne," said Amelia Bedelia. Ms. Garcia had already filled in Mrs. Hawthorne about the broken incubator, so when Amelia Bedelia told her about the spring fair they were having to raise money for a new one, Mrs. Hawthorne was delighted to help out.

"Which animals would you like?" Mrs. Hawthorne asked.

"I was thinking bunnies and duckies," said Amelia Bedelia.

"Sounds great," said Mrs. Hawthorne. "There's just one catch. We'll be at a family wedding. So you'll have to pick them up yourself. Will that be possible?"

"I'm pretty good at catching," Amelia Bedelia said.

"All righty, then," said Mrs. Hawthorne. "I hope you get a real kick out of the babies!"

"The bunnies, maybe," said Amelia Bedelia.

After they'd worked out the details, Amelia Bedelia hung up. "Mom, guess what!" she said. "Mrs. Hawthorne is loaning us her baby rabbits and ducklings for the petting zoo. We're going to need to pick them up ourselves. She asked if we had a trailer."

"A trailer?" said her mother. "Maybe you heard her wrong. Bunnies and duckies don't take up that much room. If I put down the back seat, we'll have plenty of space."

Amelia Bedelia started thinking. "I know! I'll bring my old wading pool for the ducklings," she said. "And I'll ask Mr. Jack if he can make us a pen for the bunnies."

Amelia Bedelia's mother smiled at her. "I'm impressed," she said. "You are really taking the bull by the horns!"

Amelia Bedelia laughed. "I don't think so, Mom. I'm pretty sure no one wants to pet a bull."

An Incubator
That Re-Fuses to Die

The door to Mr. Jack's office was open, and his back was turned. Amelia Bedelia stood in the doorway for a moment, taking it all in. Mr. Jack's office had a desk, but it looked more like a den. Her father would love it. There was a TV, a refrigerator, a couch, a worktable, and a recliner. The room was cluttered with tools, paint and supplies, and books.

"Knock, knock," said Amelia Bedelia, lightly rapping her knuckles on the door frame.

"Hop on in, Amelia Bedelia," said Mr. Jack. He stood up from his stool, wiping his hands on a rag, and began clearing a place for her to sit, stacking newspapers, woodworking magazines, and catalogs into a big pile. "Have a seat," he said.

"Thanks, Mr. Jack," said Amelia Bedelia. "I don't mean to interrupt you. We were just wondering if you could help us with—" Just then she spotted the broken incubator on Mr. Jack's worktable. "Are you fixing it?" she asked.

"It's finished," said Mr. Jack, nodding.

Amelia Bedelia sighed. "I figured it would be," she said. "It's okay, though, because we came up with a plan to get a new one."

"It's all done," said Mr. Jack, gently patting the top of the incubator.

That was when Amelia Bedelia noticed something odd. "Why is there a light on inside?" she asked.

"It will help to keep them warm," said Mr. Jack.

"Who's *them*?" asked Amelia Bedelia.

"The baby chicks. Hopefully," said Mr. Jack. "I'm getting some eggs to test it out."

Amelia Bedelia was in a daze. They had all assumed that the incubator was beyond repair.

"You mean it works?" said Amelia Bedelia.

"So far," said Mr. Jack. "It just needed a little tune-up and some spit and polish."

"Spit?" Amelia Bedelia could not help herself. She stared at Mr. Jack. They did not call him a jack-of-all-trades for nothing! "You're the best, Mr. Jack!" she said.

"Why, thank you, Amelia Bedelia." said Mr. Jack.

"When you said it was finished, I thought it was—"

"Ancient? On its last legs?" he said. "Oh no. You see, sometimes old things are the best things, and all they need is a little elbow grease."

"You fixed the incubator with spit *and*

elbow grease?" Amelia Bedelia shook her head in disbelief.

Mr. Jack laughed. "Mostly just a little tender loving care," he said. "And a new fuse."

"Our class will be so happy that you fixed our incubator, especially Ms. Garcia," said Amelia Bedelia.

"She may not like to admit it, but Ms. Garcia was in the third grade when this incubator was delivered to the school," said Mr. Jack. "I'll never forget the look on her face when those chicks started to hatch. She was more excited than if you'd given her a check for a million dollars."

Amelia Bedelia tried hard to imagine Ms. Garcia as a student at Oak Tree

Elementary and what it would have been like to sit next to her in science class. She leaned over to get a closer look at the incubator.

"Are we the only ones who know the incubator is working?" asked Amelia Bedelia.

"Just us two chickens," said Mr. Jack.

"Maybe we should keep it a secret for now," said Amelia Bedelia. "I mean, we don't want to cancel the spring fair. Everything is all set up! Plus, you're still testing it, right?"

"Amelia Bedelia, my lips are sealed," said Mr. Jack.

A Taste of Holland

The next morning Ms. Garcia met them at the door with a big smile on her face.

"Did Harriet come home?" Rose asked.

Ms. Garcia shook her head. "Not yet," she said. "But she keeps coming back every night for her food. So I think it's just a matter of time!"

"Then why are you so happy?" asked Pat.

"Well, I know you probably wanted to keep it a surprise, but Mrs. Shauk let the cat out of the bag this morning."

Amelia Bedelia gasped. Had Mr. Jack forgotten to seal his lips? Had he told Mrs. Shauk? Can a cat be put back in a bag?

Ms. Garcia continued, "She mentioned the spring fair you are putting together to raise the money for a new incubator."

Whew! Amelia Bedelia raised her hand. "Just so you know, there aren't going to be any cats in the petting zoo," she explained. "Or bulls."

Ms. Garcia nodded. "Thank you for

clarifying that, Amelia Bedelia. And I can help you all out in any way you need at the fair. Just let me know what I can do." She beamed at the class. "I'm just so proud of you all I could burst my buttons."

Amelia Bedelia was alarmed. She kept a close watch on Ms. Garcia for the entire class. Thankfully, her buttons stayed in place.

After school, Amelia Bedelia took Finally for a walk. They headed for the park, but before they got there, they made a right on Larkspur Lane. Amelia Bedelia knew where she was going. She and Finally were soon standing in front of a small yellow house with a garden. Not just any garden—the entire yard was a sea of brightly colored tulips and daffodils. Everyone in the neighborhood called it Little Holland, after the part of the Netherlands where the owner, Mrs. Van Dyke, came from. But what Amelia Bedelia liked the most were her lawn ornaments. An elegant birdbath. A windmill that really spun. A wishing well. And best of all, a garden gnome named Sven. He had a white beard and a red hat and was holding a watering can as he surveyed the yard. From the look on his face, he approved.

Everyone said that Mrs. Van Dyke had a green thumb. Amelia Bedelia had never seen it because Mrs. Van Dyke's hands were always covered by garden gloves. Mrs. Van Dyke had short snow-white hair and twinkling blue eyes behind large pink glasses. She reminded Amelia Bedelia of Mrs. Claus. In addition to being a master gardener, she was also a world-class baker who shared her tasty treats with her neighbors.

"Hello! Mrs. Van Dyke?" called Amelia Bedelia, ringing the little garden bell.

Mrs. Van Dyke popped up from behind the wishing well. She was wearing a baby-blue jumpsuit and an oversized straw hat and pink rubber clogs. "Well, hello there, Amelia Bedelia," she said. "Come right in."

Amelia Bedelia opened the gate and stepped into Little Holland.

"Those grew from bulbs I planted last

fall," said Mrs. Van Dyke, pointing out her latest tulips, their beautiful heads bobbing in the breeze.

Amelia Bedelia stared at Mrs. Van Dyke. "From the *what* you planted last fall?" she asked.

"Bulbs," replied Mrs. Van Dyke.

"Light bulbs?" said Amelia Bedelia, her eyes wide.

Mrs. Van Dyke nodded. "They certainly weren't heavy," she said.

"That is amazing," said Amelia Bedelia. She was going to tell her parents. Maybe their house could be a mini Holland next spring!

"Oh, heavens," Mrs. Van Dyke cried. "Where are my manners? I have a plate

of freshly baked cookies on my counter!"

Mrs. Van Dyke scurried inside. Amelia Bedelia hoped she'd find her manners there. But she really hoped she would remember to bring back cookies too. She was relieved when Mrs. Van Dyke returned with a plate piled high.

"Here you go," Mrs. Van Dyke said proudly, setting the plate on a giant ceramic toadstool. "Stroopwafels!"

"Bless you!" said Amelia Bedelia. That's what her mother said when someone sneezed.

"Thank you," said Mrs. Van Dyke.

"What are stroopwafels?" asked Amelia Bedelia.

"A treat from my homeland, the

Netherlands," said Mrs. Van Dyke. "It's a sandwich cookie—two thin waffles with caramel in between. Try one!"

Amelia Bedelia never had to be asked twice when offered a cookie. She selected one and took a bite. "*Mmmmm! Delicious!*" She took another bite. It was so amazing that Amelia Bedelia just had to ask. "Mrs. Van Dyke, we're having a spring fair at school on Saturday to raise money to buy a new incubator for baby chicks. Would you please donate a batch of stroopwafels to our bake sale?"

"I'd be pleased as punch!" said Mrs. Van Dyke.

"We're okay for punch," said Amelia

Bedelia. "But your stroopwafels will be a big hit!"

Amelia Bedelia wondered if Saturday would ever come. When the last bell rang on Friday afternoon, she and her friends actually cheered. It was time to set up their spring fair.

They went to the cafeteria and got to work. Candy sat at a table with a big glass jar and an enormous bag of jelly beans. She began dropping them into the jar, counting each one as she did. Meanwhile, everyone else began opening the plastic eggs and filling them with chocolate eggs and gummy chicks and bunnies.

"What kind of beans don't grow in a garden?" Clay asked.

"Jelly beans!" everyone shouted back.

"Hey, Wade," said Heather. "You're eating more candy than you're putting in the eggs."

"I've only had seven pieces!" argued Wade. "Or maybe eight. Okay maybe twelve, but that's it!" He shrugged. "Hey, I'm hungry!"

Candy groaned. "Please stop blurting out numbers while I'm counting jelly beans. You distracted me. Now I have to start over. With a sigh, she dumped the jelly beans from the jar back into the bag and started over.

When the jelly beans had all been

counted (seven hundred and sixty-seven, which Ms. Garcia carefully wrote down) and all the eggs had been filled, a few kids went outside to hide them. They tucked them in the crooks of trees, under the bushes that lined the walkways, by the swing set, in flower beds. Amelia Bedelia found a little hollow in a tree and put one of the eggs in there. It seemed like a great hiding place. She just hoped a squirrel wouldn't find it first.

After all the eggs were hidden, everyone helped Clay and Cliff set up the obstacle course. There were planters to jump over, buckets and watering cans to weave around, a bench to crawl under, and a wagon full of rocks to pull a short

distance. They even incorporated the tree stump table (to climb over) and the tire swing (to crawl through) as part of the course.

Cliff pointed to the huge pile of bunny ears and cotton tails next to the BUNNY HOP OBSTACLE COURSE sign.

"Only two people can do the obstacle course at a time," he said. "So what are we going to do with all these extra ears and tails?"

"I'm sure we'll think of something," said Mrs. Shauk.

Joy helped Daisy, Penny, Wade, Skip, and Pat set up the games and activities. There was a ring toss game, face painting, a photo booth, the egg-and-spoon race, a rubber duck matching game, and a bean bag throw. They were going to set up a hat-decorating table too, and Jackie from the Upcycling Art Studio had agreed to bring her best trash treasure to decorate with. And Joy's sister had promised to bring the high school marching band to lead the parade!

Last but not least, Amelia Bedelia set up the petting zoo with her wading pool from home and the pen Mr. Jack had built for the bunnies. She could already picture the ducklings paddling around. She had put the pen over the greenest grass with the most clover. She was sure the bunnies were going to be very happy.

The playground was transformed!

Now they just had to hope that lots of people showed up. They didn't want to disappoint Ms. Garcia.

No Business Like ~~Show~~ Zoo Business

On Saturday morning Amelia Bedelia and her mother drove to Seven Gables Farm.

"Do you know where to go?" asked her mother when they arrived.

"Mrs. Hawthorne said she would leave me a note at the farm stand," answered Amelia Bedelia.

And sure enough, there it was:

Amelia Bedelia and her mother followed the arrow. But where were the duckies and bunnies? There were just two baby donkeys standing in a pen, blinking their large brown eyes at them. *Hee-haw!* one of them brayed. Amelia Bedelia stepped forward to scratch his long fuzzy ear.

"Where do you think they are?" asked Amelia Bedelia.

Her mother shook her head as she surveyed the area. "No bunnies or duckies in sight," she said. "I wonder . . ." Her voice trailed off, and she suddenly burst into laughter.

"What's so funny?' asked Amelia Bedelia.

Her mother pointed to the sign on the donkeys' pen. "I'm so sorry, cookie, but I don't think your petting zoo is going to happen. Our back seat isn't big enough!"

Amelia Bedelia stared at the sign on the donkeys' enclosure. It read:

BUNNY AND DUCKIE

Mrs. Hawthorne hadn't been talking about ducklings and bunnies. She was lending Amelia Bedelia her baby donkeys named Duckie and Bunny!

"You have to admit, as far as misunderstandings go, this one is pretty funny," her mother said as they got back into the car. "Those foals are adorable!"

Amelia Bedelia shook her head. She didn't have to admit anything. She sighed.

"Everyone is going to be so disappointed," she said as they drove toward the school. How was she going to face her friends without animals for the petting zoo? Her mother made a right onto Main Street, and they drove past the animal shelter. Amelia Bedelia could see Dr. Wiggins heading inside.

"The puppies!" she shouted. "That's it!"

"What's it?" said her mother.

"Stop the car, Mom!" she yelled. Her mother glanced at her. "I mean, please stop the car, Mom."

Dr. Wiggins gazed down at the petting zoo, which now had a sign that said PETTING ZOO + PET ADOPTION, with a huge smile on her face. "What an amazing idea you had," she said to Amelia Bedelia. "And thank goodness I had some extra puppy pens."

The puppies from the animal shelter were wiggling and rolling and playing. Each puppy wore bunny ears and a cotton tail—at least for now! Cliff and Clay had given Amelia Bedelia some of their extras.

The petting zoo was popular! The line was super long. Amelia Bedelia ran the petting zoo part, and Dr. Wiggins had set up a table for the adoption paperwork. She was very busy.

A bit later Ms. Crabtree and a few volunteers from the animal shelter showed up to help, and Amelia Bedelia took a break. People were lining up for the obstacle course, buying treats from the bake sale, taking silly photos, getting their faces painted, racing with eggs on spoons, submitting guesses for the jelly bean count. Lots of people had shown up in funny hats for the parade that would close the fair.

Amelia Bedelia smiled. Things were going better than expected. She really hoped that the old incubator passed Mr. Jack's test, but if it didn't, they were going to raise a ton of money for a new one!

Amelia Bedelia could hear Dawn over the loudspeaker. "Five minutes to the egg hunt! The egg hunt will start in five minutes!"

"Come on," she said, grabbing Joy by the hand. "The egg hunt is about to start. You're really good at noticing things that other people miss. I bet you'll find a ton!"

They joined the large group gathered around Rose and Dawn. "Welcome to the egg hunt!" Dawn announced. "The hunt will begin when Rose blows the whistle. Don't worry, there are plenty of eggs for everyone!"

TWEET!

Charge! The crowd surged forward, nearly knocking a couple of kids to the ground. Once the stampede was over, Amelia Bedelia was dashing here and there hunting for eggs. Joy stayed in the same spot, turning around and around to see what she could see.

After the egg hunt had been going on for ten minutes, eggs were getting harder and harder to find. Even though Amelia Bedelia had helped to hide a few eggs, she couldn't remember exactly where she'd hidden them! She was happy to count twelve eggs in her basket. She hoped they were filled with chocolate. But when she glanced over at Joy, she felt really bad. Joy's basket was completely empty. Amelia Bedelia had dragged her over to be her partner, and now Joy had nothing to show for it.

"Don't worry, Joy," she said. "I'll share mine with you."

"What is that?" asked Joy.

"What is what?" said Amelia Bedelia.

"*That,*" said Joy. "That right there." She pointed to the tree closest to the building. She began walking quickly toward it. Amelia Bedelia was almost running to keep up. She spotted an egg in a bush as they passed. "Hey, Joy! There's an egg you can—"

But Joy kept going. When they got to the tree, Joy reached up, trying to grab the lowest branch.

"I could use another foot," said Joy. "I'm not tall enough."

"I can't help with that," said Amelia Bedelia. "But I can give you a boost."

"Deal," said Joy. Amelia Bedelia joined her hands together, interlacing her fingers, and bent down.

"Okay, I'll count to three and then up you go," said Amelia Bedelia. "One, two, three!"

"Got it!" said Joy, grabbing the branch and pulling herself up.

Soon Amelia Bedelia could barely spot her friend through the branches covered in white and pink blossoms.

"Come here, you rascal, you," said Joy. "*Shhhh. Shhhh.* It's okay. I got you."

Who was Joy talking to?

"I'm coming back down," Joy called. She swung from branch to branch until she reached the lowest one. Then she hung there for a minute before dropping to the ground. Blossoms fell like snow all around her.

Amelia Bedelia put her hand under Joy's arm and helped her up. That was when she saw something moving around in Joy's sweatshirt.

"What *is* that?" said Amelia Bedelia.

"She's an old friend of ours." Joy reached into her sweatshirt pocket. "Amelia Bedelia, say hello to Harriet!"

Homecoming for Harriet

After the egg hunt and the hat parade, the spring fair began to wind down. Ms. Garcia stood in front of the crowd, holding the giant jar of jelly beans. "Before I announce the winner of the jelly bean count, I want to thank you all for coming to our spring fair," she announced. "We are so lucky to have such a supportive community. We loved watching our friends and neighbors having a wonderful time while raising money for a good cause. Thanks to you, now our school will be able to purchase a brand-new top-of-the-line incubator. Our school will be hatching baby chicks and learning about science and nature for years to come!"

Everyone applauded.

"And special thanks go to Mrs. Shauk's class," Ms. Garcia continued. "They worked really hard to pull this event together. Not only that, the festivities were irresistible to our favorite climber. No, not Joy—Harriet! I'm happy to announce that Harriet the hamster is back!"

Everyone cheered again, Amelia Bedelia and her friends loudest of all.

Dr. Wiggins stepped forward. "I'm grateful to Amelia Bedelia for her idea to bring the puppies from the animal shelter to the spring fair. Thanks to you all, they are all being adopted into good homes. Each and every one!"

Amelia Bedelia felt a tap on her shoulder. She turned around. It was her mother and father. They each gave her a big hug.

"We're proud of you and your friends, honey bun," her mother whispered in her ear.

Ms. Garcia then announced the winner of the jelly bean count. "Brian McAndrew,

125

everyone's favorite accountant, with an absolutely correct guess of seven hundred and sixty-seven!"

Amelia Bedelia's father laughed. "It figures that the professional bean counter won!"

Dr. Wiggins walked over to them, a huge smile on her face. "I was worried about all those puppies. I'm so happy they all have found their furever homes. Amelia Bedelia, you are one in a million."

Ms. Garcia turned around. "Tell me something I don't know," she said.

When no one said anything, Amelia Bedelia decided to speak up. "Okay," she said. "Dr. Wiggins's full name is Ernestine Dedication Wiggins."

Dr. Wiggins frowned. "That's news to me," she said.

"Well, you told me that Dedication was your middle name," said Amelia Bedelia.

Everyone was quiet for a moment, then burst into laughter. It had been a wonderful day full of fun and surprises—rescuing Harriet, figuring out how to save the petting zoo, and then finding homes for the puppies . . . and maybe the most exciting thing, the promise of an incubator (maybe two—shhh!) full of fluffy yellow chicks. So even though Amelia Bedelia wasn't exactly sure what was so funny, she was so happy that she laughed the loudest of them all.

"I Don't Want to Hear a *PEEP* Out of You!"

Spring was in the air when Amelia Bedelia walked to school on Monday morning. She hopped on her right foot. Then she hopped on her left. She hopped past Mr. Jack, who was filling the bird feeder in front of the building.

"Hi, Mr. Jack!" said Amelia Bedelia.

"Is today the day?"

"I say we spring into action," said Mr. Jack. "Come with me."

Amelia Bedelia followed Mr. Jack to his office. There was the old incubator, humming softly on the table. "Is it working?" she asked.

"It's as fit as a fiddle," said Mr. Jack.

"Is that why it's humming?" asked Amelia Bedelia.

"Could be," said Mr. Jack. "Could be."

Very carefully, Amelia Bedelia and Mr. Jack carried the old incubator to Ms. Garcia's classroom and set it down gently on a table in front of the class.

"Good morning, Mr. Jack," said Ms. Garcia. "What have we here?"

There was a muffled *Peep!*

A funny look came over Ms. Garcia's face. "What was that?"

"No way!" said Clay.

"Way!" said Cliff.

Amelia Bedelia's friends all rushed to the front of the room, surrounding the incubator.

Peep! Peep!

Ms. Garcia's eyes were darting here and there, looking everywhere. "Will someone please check Harriet?" she asked. "Is she okay?"

Peep!

Actually, that peep had come from Clay. He had done it on purpose, just to annoy Ms. Garcia.

"Aha," she said. "Clay is the culprit."

She was looking straight at him when a new round of peeps pinged through the air. *Peep! Peep! Peep!*

A look of confusion came over Ms. Garcia's face. "Clay, how are you doing that without moving your lips? Anyway, if I hear one more peep out of you, you are going to the principal's—"

Peep!

"That does it," said Ms. Garcia.

"Well now, hold on," said Mr. Jack. "I remember back when we got our first batch of chicks to hatch in this incubator. You were in the third grade and so excited that you kept racing around the room yelling, 'THE

CHICKIES ARE COMING!' Finally your teacher sent you to the principal's office."

Amelia Bedelia and her friends looked at one another, eyes wide. It was almost impossible to imagine their science teacher doing that.

"I don't remember, but it sounds like me at that age," said Ms. Garcia. She laughed. "We aren't spring chickens anymore."

"No, but they are," said Mr. Jack, lifting the lid of the incubator.

A chorus of peeps filled the air. Mr. Jack scooped up one chick, cradled it for a second, then handed the soft golden ball of fluff to Ms. Garcia.

"This is the best gift I have ever

gotten," said Ms. Garcia. "Thank you!"

"It's so great that you recycled that old incubator, Mr. Jack," said Joy. "Now we don't have to take it to the dump."

"Plus we can use the money we raised for something else," said Wade.

"Like what?" asked Holly.

Amelia Bedelia and her friends had a lot of ideas, including a pizza party for the entire school, making a donation to the animal shelter, bringing Duckie and Bunny to school as new class pets, buying seeds for the Hawthornes' farm, purchasing new books for the school library, getting a super fast slide for the playground. . . .

"You can save it for a rainy day," suggested Mr. Jack.

"It's always good to have a nest egg," added Ms. Garcia. "Come rain or come shine."

A nest egg. That made perfect sense to Amelia Bedelia. But just until they hatched a great new plan!

Two Ways to Say It

Search me!

I don't know.

She struck pay dirt.

She found something valuable.

Have a hollow leg.

Can eat or drink a lot.

Bend over backward.

Put in a lot of effort.

I am happy as a clam.

I am very, very happy.

I have spring fever.

I am restless and excited.

Let's get the ball rolling!

Let's get started!

She's pleased as punch.

She's very happy.

Taking the bull by the horns.

Taking control of a problem.

He let the cat out of the bag.

He revealed the secret.

Springtime

Tools:
scissors
stapler

Supplies:
tissue paper
pipe cleaners

Tips:

- Experiment with your tissue paper!

- You can use one tissue paper color or you can combine colors for multicolored petals.

- The bigger your sheets of tissue paper, the bigger your flower.

- The more layers you put in your stack, the more petals you will have.

Flowers

Directions

1. Cut your tissue paper into same-size sheets, rectangles or squares, anywhere from 5 inches to 12 inches wide.

2. Stack 4-5 sheets into a neat pile.

3. Starting at one end, fold the entire stack accordion style. Make your folds about 1 inch wide.

4. Staple the folded stack in the center.

5 Use scissors to shape both ends of the stack. This will change the shape of your flower.

Frilly edges

Wavy edges

OP design your own!

Rounded edges

Pointed edges

6 Wrap one end of the pipe cleaner tightly around the center of the stack. This is your stem.

7 Gently pull apart the tissue paper layers one by one.

8

FLUFF!

Optional:

- You can make a garland by attaching the flowers to a string or long ribbon.

- Or arrange your flowers in a vase.

- Or make a flower bouquet and tie it with a ribbon.

Happy Spring!

Amelia Bedelia's April Fools
SWEET SLIDERS AND FRIES
This recipe makes 12 sliders

Is it the main course, or dessert?

Ingredients

For the sliders:
24 small round vanilla cookies

12 small chocolate-covered mint patties

½ tub of vanilla frosting

12 orange or yellow fruity chew candies

2 tablespoons shredded coconut

½ teaspoon sesame seeds

8–10 drops red food coloring

8–10 drops drops green food coloring

1 teaspoon honey

For the fries:
Pound cake

Red frosting from sliders

Directions

1. Arrange 12 vanilla cookies, flat side up, on a plate or cookie sheet. Set 12 more to the side.

2. Spoon half the frosting into a piping bag or sealable baggie. Add 8–10 drops of red food coloring, seal the bag, and squeeze gently until color is fully mixed.

3. Snip a corner of the bag and pipe a dab of frosting (ketchup) on each of the first 12 cookies (bun).

4. Place one mint patty (burger) on top of the dab of frosting.

5. Place 2–3 fruity chew candies at a time on a plate, and microwave for 5 seconds, until slightly softened.

6. Cover the candies with waxed paper or foil and use a rolling pin to roll the candies until they are large enough to cover the patties.

7. Place a flattened fruit candy (cheese) on each mint patty.

8. Pipe a bit of "ketchup" on top of the "cheese."

9. Place the shredded coconut into another sealable baggie and add 8–10 drops of green food coloring. Shake until all coconut is green.

10. Sprinkle the coconut (lettuce) on top of the "ketchup."

11. Cover with another vanilla cookie, flat side down (top bun).

12. Using a clean paintbrush or pastry brush, brush the top of the "bun" with honey. (Add a couple of drops of water to the honey if necessary.)

13. Sprinkle sesame seeds on top.

14. For the fries, slice several pieces from the pound cake and cut into French fry–sized strips.

15. Put in toaster oven or regular oven until lightly toasted.

16. Place on plate next to sliders, with red frosting "ketchup" for dipping.

Ask a grown-up to help with the oven and microwave!

BONUS: Undrinkable Juice

Prepare fruit-flavored gelatin mix according to instructions on the packet and pour the liquid into drinking glasses. Put a paper straw into each glass before placing in refrigerator to set (at least half an hour). Once gelatin is solid, serve alongside the sliders and fries.

April Fools'!

The Amelia Bedelia Chapter Books

 **1** *Amelia Bedelia Means Business*
by Herman Parish, pictures by Lynne Avril

 **2** *Amelia Bedelia Unleashed*
by Herman Parish, pictures by Lynne Avril

 **3** *Amelia Bedelia Road Trip!*
by Herman Parish, pictures by Lynne Avril

 **4** *Amelia Bedelia Goes Wild!*
by Herman Parish, pictures by Lynne Avril

 **5** *Amelia Bedelia Shapes Up*
by Herman Parish, pictures by Lynne Avril

 **6** *Amelia Bedelia Cleans Up*
by Herman Parish, pictures by Lynne Avril

Have you read them all?

7 Amelia Bedelia Sets Sail
by Herman Parish · pictures by Lynne Avril

8 Amelia Bedelia Dances Off
by Herman Parish · pictures by Lynne Avril

9 Amelia Bedelia On the Job
by Herman Parish · pictures by Lynne Avril

10 Amelia Bedelia Ties the Knot
by Herman Parish · pictures by Lynne Avril

11 Amelia Bedelia Makes a Splash
by Herman Parish · pictures by Lynne Avril

12 Amelia Bedelia Digs In
by Herman Parish · pictures by Lynne Avril

Amelia Bedelia & FRIENDS

1 Amelia Bedelia & FRIENDS
Beat the Clock
by Herman Parish   pictures by Lynne Avril

2 Amelia Bedelia & FRIENDS
The Cat's Meow
by Herman Parish   pictures by Lynne Avril

3 Amelia Bedelia & FRIENDS
Arise and Shine
by Herman Parish   pictures by Lynne Avril

Amelia Bedelia & FRIENDS
Paint the Town
by Herman Parish   pictures by Lynne Avril
4

5 Amelia Bedelia & FRIENDS
Mind Their Manners
by Herman Parish   pictures by Lynne Avril

Amelia Bedelia & FRIENDS
Blast Off!
by Herman Parish   pictures by Lynne Avril
6